THE BIGGEST PUMPKIN EVER!

by Elizabeth Bennett
Illustrated by Liza Woodruff

Scholastic Inc.
New York   Toronto   London   Auckland   Sydney
Mexico City   New Delhi   Hong Kong   Buenos Aires

To Noreen, who has the biggest heart ever!
— E.B.

For Bay and Tess.
— L.W.

ISBN-13: 978-0-545-00232-5
ISBN-10: 0-545-00232-X

12 11 10 9 8 7 6 5 4 3 2   7 8 9 10 11 12/0

Printed in the U.S.A.
First printing, October 2007

Every year near Halloween,
my village holds the Pumpkin Scene.

This year I will win the prize.
I'll grow a pumpkin, giant-sized.

My brothers say that I'm too small.
They do not want my help at all.

I plant a seed and tend with care.
My pumpkin needs both sun and air.

I hope to watch it grow and grow.

Oh, no!

Again I try to plant some seeds.
I clear the ground of rocks and weeds.

I hope to watch it grow and grow.

Oh, no!

One last time I plant a seed.
A single pumpkin's all I need.

I hope to watch it grow and grow.

Oh, no!

The leaves have changed.
I feel a chill.

I take a walk toward
the backyard hill.

Whoa!

I'm so smart, so very clever.
I grew the biggest pumpkin ever!